MAX LUCADO'S
HeRMIe
& Friends

The 12 Bugs of Christmas

Story by Troy Schmidt
Illustrations by GlueWorks Animation

Based on the characters from Max Lucado's
Hermie: A Common Caterpillar

Tommy
NELSON

www.tommynelson.com

A Division of Thomas Nelson, Inc.
www.ThomasNelson.com

Published in Nashville, Tennessee, by Tommy Nelson®, a Division of Thomas Nelson, Inc.

Library of Congress Cataloging-in-Publication Data

Schmidt, Troy.
    12 Bugs of Christmas / story by Troy Schmidt ; illustrations by Glue Works Animation.
        p. cm.
    "Max Lucado's Hermie and Friends."
    ISBN 1-4003-0491-1 (picture book)

                                                                                    2004014210

Printed in China
04 05 06 07 08 SF 5 4 3 2 1

When the wise men saw the star, they were filled with joy. They went to the house where the child was and saw him with his mother, Mary. They bowed down and worshiped the child. They opened the gifts they brought for him.

—Matthew 2:10–11

On the first day of Christmas
a nice bug gave to me

A Hermie and a Wormie.

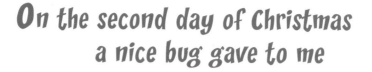

On the second day of Christmas
a nice bug gave to me

2 butterflies,

And a Hermie and a Wormie.

On the third day of Christmas
a nice bug gave to me

3 ladybugs,

2 butterflies,
And a Hermie and a Wormie.

On the fourth day of Christmas
a nice bug gave to me

4 Water Beetles,

3 ladybugs,
2 butterflies,
And a Hermie and a Wormie.

4 Water Beetles,
3 ladybugs,
2 butterflies,
And a Hermie and a Wormie.

On the sixth day of Christmas
a nice bug gave to me

6 spiders spinning,

5 ants that sing,
4 Water Beetles,
3 ladybugs,
2 butterflies,
And a Hermie and a Wormie.

On the seventh day of Christmas
a nice bug gave to me

7 snails a-slimin',

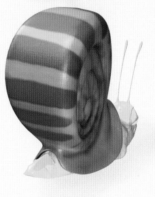

Rockefella Square

6 spiders spinning,
5 ants that sing,
4 Water Beetles,
3 ladybugs,
2 butterflies,
And a Hermie and a Wormie.

On the eighth day of Christmas
a nice bug gave to me

8 fleas a-scratchin',

7 snails a-slimin',
6 spiders spinning,
5 ants that sing,
4 Water Beetles,
3 ladybugs,
2 butterflies,
And a Hermie and a Wormie.

On the ninth day of Christmas
a nice bug gave to me

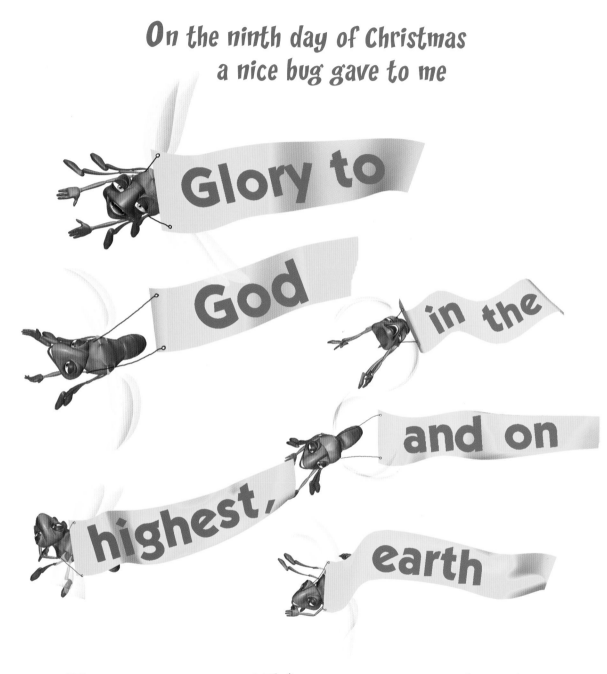

Glory to God in the highest, and on earth

9 dragonflies a-flyin',

peace,

goodwill

toward men!

8 fleas a-scratchin',
7 snails a-slimin',
6 spiders spinning,
5 ants that sing,
4 Water Beetles,
3 ladybugs,
2 butterflies,
And a Hermie and a Wormie.

On the tenth day of Christmas
a nice bug gave to me

10 bees so busy,

9 dragonflies a-flyin',
8 fleas a-scratchin',
7 snails a-slimin',
6 spiders spinning,
5 ants that sing,
4 Water Beetles,
3 ladybugs,
2 butterflies,
And a Hermie and a Wormie.

On the eleventh day of Christmas
a nice bug gave to me

11 flies a-buzzin',

10 bees so busy,
9 dragonflies a-flyin',
8 fleas a-scratchin',
7 snails a-slimin',
6 spiders spinning,
5 ants that sing,
4 Water Beetles,
3 ladybugs,
2 butterflies,
And a Hermie and a Wormie.

On the twelfth day of Christmas
a nice bug gave to me

12 caterpillars prayin',

11 flies a-buzzin',
10 bees so busy,
9 dragonflies a-flyin',
8 fleas a-scratchin',
7 snails a-slimin',
6 spiders spinning,
5 ants that sing,
4 Water Beetles,
3 ladybugs,
2 butterflies,
And a Hermie and a Wormie.